Disney's Aladdin

Monkey Business

Story by Barbara Bazaldua
Illustrated by Don Williams

A GOLDEN BOOK • NEW YORK
Western Publishing Company, Inc., Racine, Wisconsin 53404

Late one afternoon a poor orphaned youth named
Aladdin was wandering alone through the bustling
marketplace of Agrabah. People hurried past him as he
searched for something to eat. Women gossiped in the
square while their children played tag around the stalls.
The vendors joked together.

Aladdin heard a young man invite his friends to
dinner. But no one spoke to Aladdin. No one invited *him.*
"I wish I had a friend," he said with a sigh as he snatched
up a crust of bread someone had dropped in the street.

Suddenly Aladdin heard a pitiful cry. He looked down and saw a little monkey peeking out from under a basket. A broken rope hung from a collar around its neck.

"You look lost and hungry," Aladdin said. He held out the crust. Shyly, the monkey crept out and took the bread. Aladdin stroked the animal's soft fur. "I wish I could keep you," he said, "but I can hardly feed myself!"

Aladdin turned to go, but before he had walked ten
steps, he felt something tug at his pants leg. The
monkey! With a mischievous grin, it scrambled onto
Aladdin's shoulder and held out a shiny red apple.

Aladdin grinned back. "You're a cute little scamp," he
said with a chuckle, "but I can't keep you."

Just then a fruit seller ran up to them, shouting, "Thief, thief! You stole my apple!"

"The monkey took it," Aladdin said. "He didn't mean any harm."

Aladdin returned the apple, but the man was still angry. "Get out of here before I call the palace guards and have you thrown into prison!" he yelled.

"You almost got me arrested!" Aladdin scolded the monkey, putting it firmly on the ground. "I told you I can't keep you. Now go!"

The monkey hung its head and crept into a doorway as Aladdin hurried away, searching for something more to eat. He didn't look back—so he didn't see the monkey trailing after him.

It was almost dark when Aladdin finally found a piece of melon for his dinner. Carrying it carefully, he hurried to the rooftop of the old building that he called home.

As he ate, Aladdin gazed at the Sultan's palace in the distance. "I wonder how it feels to live in a palace like the Sultan's daughter, Princess Jasmine," Aladdin thought. "I'll bet *she* never goes to bed hungry."

With a sigh, Aladdin lay down to sleep. Suddenly a small dark shape scurried toward him. "Who's that!" Aladdin exclaimed. Then he laughed. The monkey had found him!

Aladdin smiled as the furry creature snuggled beside him. "All right, you can stay with me tonight," he said. "But tomorrow I'm taking you back to where you belong!"

The next morning Aladdin and the monkey woke up early. The streets were already lined with people. Aladdin elbowed his way through the crowds until he came to the city gates.

A huge caravan was just coming through. "Make way for Prince Hakin," the caravan guards shouted. "He's come to ask for Princess Jasmine's hand in marriage."

The prince's caravan filled the street. Aladdin and his little friend watched as camels and donkeys loaded down with treasure shuffled by. Then came animal trainers with cages of monkeys, birds, and other exotic creatures for Princess Jasmine's menagerie.

Suddenly the monkey in Aladdin's arms began shaking and squealing with fright. He made such a ruckus that one of the animal trainers turned to see what was going on.

"Hey! That's my monkey!" the trainer yelled at Aladdin. "It ran away yesterday! Give it back!"

As the monkey tried to scamper under Aladdin's
vest, the trainer swung his heavy walking stick at the
frightened animal. "That monkey is mine," he snarled.
"Hand him over!"

"No! Not if you're going to beat him," Aladdin replied.

"Help! He stole my monkey!" the trainer shouted,
pointing at Aladdin. "Call the guards!"

Quickly, Aladdin scooped up a handful of dust and blew it in the trainer's face.

"AAAAA-choo!" the trainer sneezed.

Aladdin turned and ran. "Come back here, you!" the trainer shouted as he took off after Aladdin.

Aladdin darted through the streets, bumping into
carts and startling camels. Rugs and lamps, baskets and
vases, fruits and vegetables tumbled to the ground
behind him.

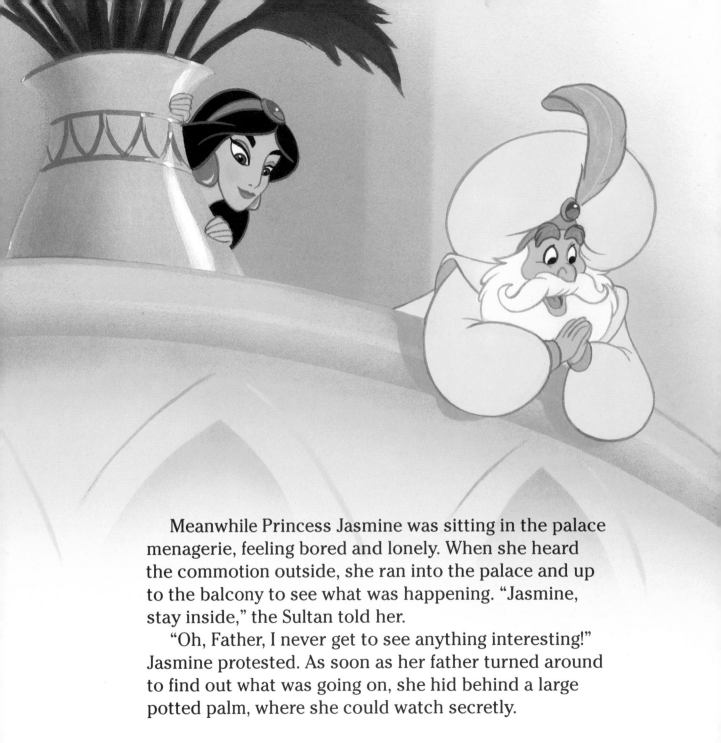

Meanwhile Princess Jasmine was sitting in the palace menagerie, feeling bored and lonely. When she heard the commotion outside, she ran into the palace and up to the balcony to see what was happening. "Jasmine, stay inside," the Sultan told her.

"Oh, Father, I never get to see anything interesting!" Jasmine protested. As soon as her father turned around to find out what was going on, she hid behind a large potted palm, where she could watch secretly.

Out in the street, Aladdin and the monkey were in trouble! The trainer was getting closer. Suddenly Aladdin saw a loose cover on one of the animal cages—and had an idea.

Clutching the monkey, Aladdin ducked under the cover and clung to the cage bars. "Hold very still," he whispered to the monkey.

Aladdin shut his eyes, held his breath, and tried not to move. Just then something warm and wet slid over his face. Aladdin opened his eyes and looked—straight into the face of a half-grown tiger cub!

The cub purred loudly. "Hush. Nice kitty . . ." Aladdin whispered.

But the cub only purred louder and licked his face
again. Aladdin tried to move away. But the tiger wanted
to play and encouraged Aladdin with a funny little
growl.

The trainer heard the noise and pulled the cover
from the cage. "Got you!" he shouted, grabbing Aladdin
by the arm.

Holding Aladdin with one hand, the trainer reached for the monkey. But the quick little creature had already scampered up the side of the cage. A big bolt held the cage door closed. The monkey yanked on the bolt, and the cage door swung open. The tiger cub sprang out.

The crowd screamed and scattered as the tiger went tearing down the street.

"Catch that tiger!" the trainer shouted. "It's a gift for the princess!" He let go of Aladdin and raced after the tiger, which was heading straight for the palace.

As soon as the trainer ran off, Aladdin darted into an alley to hide. Suddenly he heard a familiar cry. Aladdin looked back. The monkey was running after him, holding out its thin arms.

Aladdin hesitated for a moment. Then he thought, "That monkey saved me. I can't leave him now." So he picked the little animal up and raced for his rooftop home.

Luckily, no one saw Aladdin and the monkey leave the alley. The palace guards and the trainer were too busy chasing the tiger. It ran straight to the palace, scampered up a tree, and sprang onto the balcony. The tiger took one look at Jasmine and, knocking over the palm, leapt into her arms.

Princess Jasmine hugged the cub's neck. "I seem to have a new friend," she said as it licked her face. "I think I'll call you Rajah."

From the safety of his rooftop, Aladdin watched the caravan leave the city that night. It looked as if the princess had rejected another suitor.

Aladdin turned to the monkey at his side. "We saved each other," he said with a smile. "I guess we belong together now." The monkey chattered happily.

"You need a name!" Aladdin declared. "I think I'll call you Abu! Aladdin and Abu," he murmured. "At last I have a friend."